To all of my former roommates, especially
Kara, Tiffany, Doan, Sheena, and Diana
—M.P.

For Julianna
—P.K.

THIS IS A BORZOI BOOK PUBLISHED BY ALFRED A. KNOPF

Text copyright © 2018 by Miranda Paul
Jacket art and interior illustrations copyright © 2018 by Paige Keiser

All rights reserved. Published in the United States by Alfred A. Knopf, an imprint of Random House Children's Books,
a division of Penguin Random House LLC, New York.

Knopf, Borzoi Books, and the colophon are registered trademarks of Penguin Random House LLC.

Visit us on the Web! rhcbooks.com

Educators and librarians, for a variety of teaching tools, visit us at RHTeachersLibrarians.com

Library of Congress Cataloging-in-Publication Data is available upon request.
ISBN 978-0-399-55332-5 (trade) – ISBN 978-0-399-55333-2 (lib. bdg.) – ISBN 978-0-399-55334-9 (ebook)

MANUFACTURED IN CHINA
October 2018
10 9 8 7 6 5 4 3 2 1

First Edition

Random House Children's Books supports the First Amendment and celebrates the right to read.

Mia
Moves
Out

By Miranda Paul

Illustrated by Paige Keiser

Alfred A. Knopf New York

When Mia moved in, Mom and Dad had a room ready for her.
"All yours," they said.

Mia liked it, but it needed something.

Something **big.**

Something **bright.**

Something **fun.**

"Perfect," said Mia. "And all mine."

Then Brandon arrived.

The room became
half as big,
and half as bright,
but it also became TWICE as fun!
"Sharing isn't so bad," Mia said.

Then birthdays happened.

Holidays happened.

Growing happened.

And twice the **fun** brought

Twice the **noise**.

Twice the **accidents**.

Twice the **mess**.

(Which took ten times as long to clean.)

Mia waded through her brother's books.

She shoved aside his toys.

She picked up a sock that—*ew!*—wasn't a sock. . . .

This clearly wasn't her room anymore.

The solution was obvious.

"For how long?" Brandon asked.
"**Forever**," Mia said.
"Hmm," said Dad. "Forever's a long time."
"Better take a friend," said Mom.

Around the corner, Mia found a new place to stay.
It wasn't **big**,
but it was **bright**.
And it was stocked with **FUN!**

Mia was just settling in when Mom jiggled the handle.
"Mia muffin. Is my wart remover in there?"
"Gross," said Mia. "I'm outta here."

Mia spied a quiet spot at the
bottom of the stairs.
It wasn't **bright**,
but it was **big**.
And those boxes looked **FUN!**

She pried open the first lid and . . .
"Aaaah! I'm outta here!"

Mia dashed into the nearest
open space.
It wasn't **big.**
　　Or **bright.**
　　　Or **fun.**
"This won't do," she said.

Mia searched high and low,

trudged through rugged terrain,

squeezed into tight spots,

and ended up exhausted . . . with no place to relax.
Mia was out of ideas.

Then she remembered—books were full of ideas.

Her new place was big.
It was bright.
And it was fun . . .
for a while, anyway.

Mia liked it, but it needed something.
No. It needed **someone**.

"Brandon?"

"Mom, where's Brandon?"

"He moved out," said Mom.

"Maybe you can still catch him," said Dad.

Mia rushed out the door. "Brandon?! Where are you going?"

"I'm moving out," he said. "Forever."
"Hmmm," said Mia.
"Forever's a long time. Better take a friend."
She slipped her hand around his.
Just like that—she got the best idea of all.

It was amazingly big.

It was fantastically bright.

It was epically fun.

And it was all theirs.